I0572652

COPYRIGHTS

Text: © Ray Kohn 2025
Cover & Graphics: © Bill Allerton 2025
Typeset & Layout: © Ray Kohn 2025
Font: Garamon 12pt.
ISBN: 978-1-0687057-6-2
Published by Ray Kohn 2025

CONTENTS   page

Ray Kohn is an author and composer. Over 100 short stories feature in Jewish Tales Untold, A Jewish Odyssey and The Cliff Edge. Here he turns his focus upon the kaleidoscope of aspects that form the foundation stones of resistance.

THE WISDOM OF KAFKA

Listening to others conversing is a habit I acquired as a child. I would sit quietly following what they were saying and soon developed an instinct assessing who was worth hearing and who was just parroting what others had told him. Of course, although the parrot may not be bright, he would probably reflect what more influential people were telling him.

The two men did not know I could hear them as I was sitting in an adjacent booth. One of them was clearly no parrot.

"I've told my clients to hold on to their shares." His tone was that of a haughty cynic. I did not know to which shares he was referring but I wanted to hear more.

"I'm not sure he is a reliable CEO," the other man replied. He had a twangy accent, maybe from Texas.

"Oh! He is reliable," the foreigner asserted. I had no idea where he came from – maybe Australia, maybe South Africa. "You just have to understand what's driving him."

"He seems to me to be attracted to young Chinese techy entrepreneurs. Don't you think that's suspicious?"

"Of course he likes clever technical expertise. It's what he thrives on. He doesn't care where they live and work. All he wants to know is how useful their ideas could be to him."

"In the U.S. of A, we value patriotism. That's probably why I see him as so unreliable. You just don't know whether he is going to dump you for a better offer from another part of the world. Don't you find that unsettling?"

"It's only unsettling if you think he is interested in your country. But he isn't. His company is built on the understanding that nations and their leaders are just there to be used to further the interests of his businesses."

"But he cannot get far without political support. In the USA, he will come crashing down when he is seen as acting against the interests of the people, or of the President. He doesn't control our armed forces: that's entirely in the hands of our President."

"But he is in many ways more powerful than the President. He is not weighed down with the politics of having to run a country. He is free to set up anywhere he wants, and he is so rich he can buy his way into anywhere."

"Well, he seems to be nothing more than the President's lapdog to me. He does whatever he is told."

"You mean he has spent time making thousands of

Americans unemployed by destroying their jobs that existed to support fellow Americans and friends abroad."

"Wasteful government expenditure, you mean."

"Of course it was no use to him. He is happy to see American power reduced. Without the infrastructure built up over the centuries, America will be hollowed out. Then it would be harder to do anything against him in future. He will fall out with Trump, but he will retain his hold on the satellites."

"Are you suggesting that he is like some sort of pawn of the Chinese?"

"No. Of course not. He isn't interested in any one country. To him, they are all merely pieces on a chessboard. He can see that Xi is already making China into a more powerful nation than the USA. You can watch how Xi uses Putin as his fool, attacking Europe and leaving Siberian land easy to annex while he is so tied up in Ukraine. Europe itself is more than happy to accept cheaper, high-quality goods from China – just look at what's happening on the electric vehicles market. China is powering ahead while Trump thinks that petrol is irreplaceable. Now as Trump attacks America's traditional allies with tariffs and threats to invade Panama, Greenland and Canada, China quietly picks up all that the U.S loses. Musk knows where the future lies. His interest is in space, not just SpaceX, whose shares I recommend. He has satellites. Now, he has his sights set on the moon and near planets. For his ambitions, he needs support from across the world from other billionaire owners while keeping politicians away from the action fighting one another.

"But no nation could withstand the US military might. Trump has already laid out that China is a threat he will not tolerate."

"So, his first action is to threaten Panama, Greenland and Canada. That doesn't sound like someone ready to counter the growing influence and alliances China has built up in Asia, Africa, South America and Europe. To many of us who are major investors, we see Trump as essentially a local bully projected up into the White House by billionaires like Musk who want to see him there rather than anyone who might threaten their power. And like all bullies, he is a coward when it comes to facing someone as big or bigger than him. He talks big against Xi but threatens him with nothing more than a few tariffs. He dares not take him on seriously. If anything, if you look at Ukraine, he is keen to cut and run. Most investors see him fearful of being drawn into a fight he could be seen to lose. He would not survive losing face."

"Rubbish. If Trump wanted to repel Russia and ensure victory for Ukraine, he has the power to do that. But what would he gain? He sees nothing to win there."

"You are right that Russia is weak. But it is Xi who is profiting from that, and America is just seen as the waning power. Trump cannot even see the military, economic and resource benefits from a Ukrainian victory. His fear of Xi and even of Putin is too strong. He would rather pretend that taking control of Greenland which never opposed the USA in the first place shows he is still important on the world stage."

"I still think you don't understand why so many Americans voted for Trump. He is offering to make America great again by shutting out those who threaten us, Mexicans taking our jobs, Canadians and Europeans living off our military protection, Chinese goods undercutting our prices.

"These are all stories on the social media that the American public reads every day. But don't you think it odd that Musk and his billionaire friends own social media. So, the stories you read there will never reflect what I've been telling you. And that is why I'm encouraging my clients to hold onto the shares. Short-term Space X losses are neither here nor there. It's the long-term gains you win by taking control of the market itself that matters."

"Well, thanks for the tip. I don't agree with what you're saying about our President; but when it comes to money, I'll take your advice."

"Perhaps you'd like the Kafka aphorism I read that my gambler wife wrote at the front of her diary."

"What was that?"

"'In the struggle between you and the world, back the world' So, either you win the struggle, or you win your bet"

Q

Donald was ecstatic. The team he had been leading had succeeded against all the odds. Competitors from other countries as well as his own had been attempting this seemingly impossible feat. It had taken years of research and a series of much-publicised failures before he was able to present the solution – the essential attributes for the preprogrammed, biologically and psychologically perfect human or human simulacrum who could survive all and every conceivable barrier society could throw up.

The trite attempts at building such a person from their genetic make-up to their social and interpersonal skillsets had been a laughingstock over the past decade. The Russian robot 'Übermensch' with its pneumatic-powered limbs and zettabytes of stored data failed to impress the international judges appointed to assess completing claims. When Principal Judge Stella Chen held out her hand in greeting 'Übermensch' responded with a punch to the ribs that put her in hospital for a week.

A little-publicised ungainly candidate developed by an impressive joint Arab/Israeli team spoke in over twenty languages but looked like a spider. Unfortunately, the seven legs had minds of their own and spent their time constantly kicking one another until the strange animal tripped itself up and rolled upside down at Stella Chen's feet.

Donald's team took a completely different approach. They realised that the physical accomplishments of any robot or human could never withstand the most powerful forces of nature. "We are not in the business of designing a human capable of surviving an earthquake. What we should be focused on is how a human can survive anything that other humans can throw up."

"Should our ideal human be male or female?" Donald's body designer asked.

"Despite all the conflicts that rage over gender issues," Donald pontificated, "I think that will dwindle to irrelevance for our project. We must think first about how this designed human will deal with the world around them."

The team spent a great deal of time assessing how well humans had survived (or not) in a vast variety of situations. Their conclusions were put to Donald who approved of their analysis which provided the foundation stone for what he dubbed 'The Ideal Survivor'.

The Cerebral Team concocted a veritable variety of brainboxes. One of them included the capacity to defeat even the most powerful chess computers at their own game. Unfortunately, that model tended to fall into a traumatic seizure when challenged with 'calculate the square root of π'. By this time, Donald had already surmised that building a totally objective intelligent brain without preconceived notions of the world might have been a liberal, open-minded ideal but not necessarily one that could cope with anything with which it was confronted.

"We need to establish what this ideal survivor needs to have preprogrammed," he announced to the Cerebral Team. Then the Sensory Team asked what filters would be required to prevent catastrophic overload. "Can you imagine how many terabytes of information storage would be needed if our ideal was left to sense and record the detail of every single blade of grass and leaf on every tree in this garden?" Donald nodded and suggested that Sensory and Cerebral Teams work together.

After all the tests had been carried out and Donald was happy with what his teams had achieved, he called on Stella Chen.

"I think you and your panel of judges will be impressed by what we have created."

"What is your model's name?" she enquired.

"This was our seventeenth model, and we gave each a letter rather than a name," Donald explained.

"So, you've called your perfect human being Q"

"Yes, that's right."

Next day, the panel was assembled and Q stood before them, dressed formally like an American businessman."

"Please sit," Stella Chen indicated the chair behind Q. Recalling previous experience with highly intelligent robots, she half expected Q to miss the chair, collapse in a heap, and terminate the assessment before having more significant intellectual challenges presented.

But Q thanked Stella, as if he were a polite human being, and sat down without any coordination problems.

"Q, I am going to give you one or two challenging questions. I must tell you that the judges are not seeking a correct answer. In fact, there might not even be anything that could be called a correct answer. The intention is to assess how you go about evaluating what we present to you. Do you understand?"

"Yes, of course I do, Stella. Thank you. Please proceed with the challenge."

"All right. I have a newspaper headline here that suggests that the economy is stagnant because of young workers nowadays being so lazy. How would you assess this suggestion."

Q stood up to answer, as if addressing a small audience. "The assumption behind this newspaper headline is basically correct. There are other factors, of course, that harm the economy; but slovenly approaches to work by the youth of today is certainly one factor." And with that, Q sat down.

The judges looked at one another. The silence was eventually broken by Q saying, "Stella, I am waiting for the next challenge."

Stella took a deep breath and said: "Very well, let us stay on issues of the economy. I have the results of a mass survey of over one hundred thousand workers aged under twenty-five. It shows that the average hours per day worked by the young is significantly greater than those worked by older people. It also shows that despite working longer hours, even those with equivalent qualifications to those who are older, the younger workers earn a lot less even though they work harder. I am sure that you would agree that this seriously contradicts the suggestion made in the newspaper headline."

Q stood up again and addressed an imaginary mass audience. "It is a common mistake to assume that surveys are reliable. Although we all know youngsters who are slackers at work, we are asked to disbelieve the evidence of our own eyes by an academic survey, undertaken, no doubt, by intellectuals who have a point to prove." And Q sat down.

Two of the judges had a quiet word in Stella's ear before she launched her final challenge.

"Can you tell us, Q, why certain groups find that they have to work harder than others for the same rewards?"

Again, Q stood and smiled at Donald and his team members who had come to witness the examination.

"It is widely understood how certain groups hold great power. It is they who decide who is condemned to work hard and who can survive without too much effort. Although they are expert in covering their tracks – which is why you will find it hard to gather any evidence – Jewish bankers decide who can be wealthy without working whilst others are condemned to slave away to keep a meal on the family table."

Stella Chen was furious. She addressed Donald directly. "How dare you present us with this appalling example of prejudice and bigotry!"

But Donald held up his hand and demanded silence. "Listen," he said. "The challenge was to create a human or human simulacrum that could survive all challenges. We have created the perfect solution to this problem. Q survives simply by discarding all evidence that might disturb its model of the world and highlight anything that could be bent into support for its preset beliefs."

"But its statements are untrue."

"That's irrelevant. You judges might not like it, but there is no way that you will be able to throw Q off its survival formula. Q embodies the best guarantee of survival."

ACADEMIA

The advantages of an academic career cannot be overstated. In my prestigious college, I have free access to meals, comfortable rooms and the convivial company of intelligent students and fellow lecturers. I am paid to teach and publish articles expanding our understanding of society. My field of political sociology is rife with uninformed publicists. But I belong to an elite band of serious researchers making an impact upon how we live.

I was encouraged by my first book's reception, studying the mechanisms used to gain and retain power. I was flooded with requests to be a visiting lecturer at home and abroad. The faculty's prestige has been raised by my efforts. I am working on my second publication analysing the role of social media in affecting public perception of critical issues.

My colleagues say I could become a leading figure in the radical movement undermining what they see as the shaky foundations of today's power holders. I am told I may understand how their power is retained better than anyone else. I'm unsure about that: but if the cap fits, I might end up wearing it!

Susan, one of my more outspoken undergraduate students, told me that my book was too verbose. I tried not to take offence. Instead, I asked her how she would summarise what I had written. Her words repeated an old saying that I had not heard for many years. 'A millionaire was asked if he was afraid of a working-class revolution. He replied: "Not at all! We just pay one half of the working-class to fight the other half, leaving us to govern."'

The tutorial with Susan was more interesting than with students who wrote predictable essays that merely reflected my views. She believed I had not grasped how powerfully influenced all walks of life were by the interests of those in power. I asked her for examples, and she described areas about which I knew far less than her. She spoke about what she called the intentionally soporific effect of most popular music: the anodyne nature of most popular culture and art: and the mass sale of escapist literature and television so-called "drama" whose endings were always a victory for those representing people in power.

She even brought in the movements that appeared to be quite neutral when it came to who held power. She said 'assisted dying' would function merely as a means by which to cut the health and pensions budgets. "You can bet your bottom dollar that the businesses that produce the appropriate drugs will benefit even more than those whose end-of-life pain is reduced." The application or withdrawal of drugs assisting those altering their gender she saw as a massive culture war irrelevance, focusing public attention on an issue of tiny significance and so deflecting attention away from major problems in housing, health and education. She even tried to analyse defence spending to demonstrate that it was radically ineffective in creating a basis from which serious threats from abroad could be neutralised.

"Are you advocating an increase in defence expenditure?" I asked, half expecting her to deny any such thing.

"We need a massive increase along with the removal of many of the political old guard who continue to believe that our armed forces are wonderful. But they are not fit for purpose. Anyone can see that if they just look at the outdated equipment available and lack of expertise in cyberwarfare."

I noted down many of Susan's points of view. After her graduation, her own academic career seemed to be assured and our first joint publication was going ahead with simultaneous launches in America, Europe, the UK and selected English-speaking countries. Susan believed that our work formed a firm foundation for alternative policies as well as helping a radically different set of people take control of social media and key parts of the economy. The book somehow failed to make an impact.

Several critiques appeared simultaneously in academic journals as well as some areas of the popular press and social media. It was almost as if these attacks had been prepared long before the appearance of the book as they were launched on the same day as the book appeared! Worse still: Susan failed to attain a position within the university – she now sells insurance. And my meeting with the bursar next week is set to discuss whether the faculty can afford to retain my services.

DUCK

There has never been a greater circus master than Domhnall Duck. DD (as everyone knew him) created the most successful circus business in the world. As his fame grew, thousands of his circuses operated on every continent, overseen from his heavily guarded coastal retreat.

Rundown areas like Oldtown in the Rust Belt were where people had given up any hope of retrieving their previous status. In years gone by, most families had a healthy income from the man's wages. Extra money from part-time employment for the wife or older children put Oldtown in the top 10% of American income households. But with steel works closures, the flight of graduates to the cities on the east and west coasts and the failure of Washington to reverse the downward trend, it took the intervention of DD to create new hope.

The creation of circus-based activity with full audience participation was a DD trademark. Instead of shameful reliance upon social security payments, households began generating income from the social media sale of their circus antics. Despite the occasional trapeze accidents, involvement in almost all circus activities became popular – especially when every member of the family of any age could help bring in more dollars than had been seen since the era of steel. Some suspect that the ever-present danger in trapeze action and lion taming was an added attraction for some participants!

It is with great sadness that supporters witnessed the way that Leon, DD's former partner, turned traitor. Leon was a star in his own right but was convinced that his social media empire that hosted many circus acts was really what the new world order was all about. He failed to grasp the essential appeal of circus to the communities where DD was making such an impact. He believed that those with the money to buy into his social media platforms supplied the critical element because it was the source of his own immense personal wealth. DD enjoyed appearing as a clown. It was his trademark and the emotional basis of his appeal.

When Leon began to be viewed as the upstart, get-rich-quick flash boy whereas DD was regarded as the down-to-earth saviour whose own wealth had been earned by openly and unapologetically trading in the dishonest world of the international property market where he had learnt where best to position his circuses. Leon's star waned as DD dropped him as his chief advisor and began making him the figure of fun in many of the circus acts. In one celebrated case, Leon's character was the human cannonball who was made to land in a slushy pool of animal excrement. When the aptly named Stevie Cannon, who had devised this stunt, pointed out that Leon was not even American, the Rust Belt dropped him in their circus advertising campaigns.

The way that intellectuals tried to understand DD's appeal is pathetic. One Professor wrote an entire book illustrating parallels between DD's achievements and the Russian revolution! Domhnall Duck becomes Vladimir Lenin. Leon is, of course, Trotsky: whilst poor Stevie Cannon was Zinoviev – to be executed at some later date by a yet-to-emerge Stalin. The reason why such books are so pathetic is that DD is not a dictator. He is kindly old man with a cheeky grin, preferring to give our children clowns and animal trainers for entertainment rather than Leon's violent computer games.

The competition between the American Duck circus and the acrobatic circuses developed in China saw Europe becoming Ducked whilst Russia only showcased 'Mao's Miracles'. The struggle by Africa and India to develop their own circuses never took off whilst the Brazilians cleverly permitted both DD and MM to be displayed throughout the South American continent. More recently, Europeans have shown a growing liking for Chinese acrobatics whilst some Chinese in the countryside have been discovered organising clandestine clown-based action. The only territory claiming to be neutral where neither circus operates is in Australia's Northern Territory. In their attempt to regain what they regarded as their lost innocence, our aboriginal community – fearing extinction – decided to ditch televisions and Internet access altogether. But their highest profile rituals are the Dance of the Dollar and the Renminbi Wrestling competition: the winners of each are major social media stars and feature in proud government announcements made from faraway Canberra.

Like Elvis last century, followers believe that Domhnall Duck is still alive and lives, resurrected, amongst us now. By contrast no one thinks Mao still walks the Earth. The Church of the Divine Duck now has over a million members, all of whom sport a red nose as a holy sign. Mao's Miracles have remained strictly secular and, in consequence, have failed to capture the sacred ground marked out by the nine thousand Duck circus locations. When our out-of-touch politicians invited Mao's Miracles to perform on the White House lawn as a gesture of goodwill and peaceful coexistence, the Capitol building was invaded by hundreds of adolescent Ducklings determined to keep American circus traditions pure.

CORA

She fascinated me. My reputation never seemed to bother her. When she challenged me on the Go website, it was as a young Chinese player with an established reputation from the provinces. But to step up from being a 1st kyu amateur to play a 2 dan professional is not as easy as her supporters liked to portray.

We met, face-to-face in Beijing and, despite being defeated, she did not seem perturbed. On the contrary, she smiled and shook my hand, congratulated me on my victory, before quietly slipping away back home. But Xīn was such a beautiful girl. I could not get her image out of my mind for the rest of the season. My sponsor said this distracted me and put me off my game. That is possible, but I have no excuses for my poor performance against the other top players.

Her reappearance in the cadre working on the creation of artificial intelligence software meant that I saw her every day. She was an accomplished A.I. developer working beside my team focusing upon the ethical aspects of A.I. usage as our political masters were concerned about A.I. being used against the interests of the State and the people.

Soon, we were dating. I could not have been happier until she broke the news of her father's death. He had been working abroad as an acclaimed academic. He and his wife had been living apart for many years: she was in Guangdong, and he was in California. With permission to travel to America to attend his funeral, I fondly awaited her return. But she did not come back.

My colleagues were the first to notice her image on a website explaining the great advantages to be gained by using the artificial intelligence software from the company she claimed she worked for. The video had her speaking Mandarin with English subtitles. A week later, an exact replica appeared with her speaking in English with Spanish subtitles. In both videos she was introduced with an American name, Cora. (This was an obvious anglicised version of her Chinese name Xin). So, I addressed her as Cora.

There was a comments box on her website where I wrote this challenge. "I am sure you're A.I. could not win a game of Go." There was an instant response on my email account. "Time for a rematch."

My team had been heavily involved in the vitriolic disputes over the use of Artificial Intelligence. On one side, there were those who wanted universal, free access to A.I., arguing that this enabled everyone to start their explorations of any subject from a position of commonly held, deep knowledge. On the other side, the equally extreme view was that if A.I. were eradicated it would lead to a flowering of human creativity, unconstrained by the necessarily backward-looking perspectives ingrained within all A.I. programs.

Social media had become the battleground where the most contentious A.I. issues were fought out. Cora, or whatever she called herself now that she was in America, had worked alongside our team. She knew all about the disputes and could, no doubt, access A.I. to support her Go moves. I doubted that any A.I. programs could overcome a 2 dan (let alone a higher dan) player. However, if our relationship meant anything, I believed her when she texted "Let's play without A.I. assistance like we did when we first met."

The game was far more equal, and my victory was very hard won. She congratulated me and asked if I would like to come and join her at her famous Californian university. I asked why she had decided not to come home to me. The dialogue slowly petered out. Her final words were "You should come here. We have advanced in your field. Our A.I. can disentangle all the false claims made by influencers and politicians, irrespective of whether they practice in America or China. You would really love what we've done."

I will admit to being very concerned that she had turned her attention to our home politicians. I had learnt that politicians in the west were expected to lie but ours were expected to remain entirely honest for the good of the Party and the country. The following month saw new claims made by Cora. She said that there was no way that her deep understanding of social media would allow her to be influenced by the false claims and misinterpretations that flood social media. The most read content over the previous months demonstrated blanket coverage of current political leaders' statements with heavily biased comments on most online platforms. Cora claimed she knew more about the media owners and influencers than any other commentator or politician. After amassing so much damning evidence against these online billionaire publicists, Cora boasted that she could not be easily swayed

Her university had been approached to grant permission to allow Cora to contribute to the televised debate between the leading election candidates. She emailed me to say that after an undisclosed fee was paid to the Treasurer, the university agreed.

However, Cora's contribution was cut short – some thought deliberately – when circuitry fused during a power surge according to the official statement from the Department of **Computer Assisted Research Assessments (CORA)**

BRAVE NEW WORLD

Some old-timers still hanker after the planet we left behind. But we know from what we've been taught, it was time to move on. The elderly gentlemen who were pretending to manage the place could not cope with the new technology. They even claimed that the revolutionary Thought Transfer Machines were suspect! How could anyone believe that a TTM billionaire owner would want to interfere with public thought transfer?

The New World runs with far greater efficiency now TTM is used. Everyone receives the same information through the amazing Leon Satellite system so all our activity can be coordinated without annoying irregularities. One particularly obstreperous pensioner, Mister Sanders, had to be gated last week when he tried to object to a perfectly sensible order that our respected President Krasnov stated was a defence requirement. How could we protect ourselves from the old planet if they decided to launch an attack?

Sander's shouting from the steps of the long- disused Capitol building was only heard by passers-by, of whom I happened to be one. The State Guards immediately took me to a debrief where I was asked what I had heard. I told them that Sanders questioned why we would need to destroy the old planet as no one from there had issued any threats. I was interrogated to discover if I was a Sanders follower! I told the interrogator, a lovely Alaskan lady with a very soothing voice, that Sanders was obviously insane. I thought it would benefit us all if he could be locked up for his own welfare or, even better, transported back to the old planet. "Do you believe that President Krasnov's Defence budget is reasonable?" she asked me. What a question! How could I be expected to make an informed assessment about such a technically difficult subject? "If our President has made an evaluation and believes that it is in all our best interests, who am I to query it?"

"Do you realise that President Krasnov has a vast team of specialists working for the Krasnov Corporation to help him analyse these major questions?" she asked.

"Of course. How could anyone be as successful as President Krasnov without him astutely choosing the best advisers to help tackle our problems!"

My TTM is running smoothly in my apartment, and I am happy as it gives me a full picture of all we need to know. The only improvement I might suggest to those in charge is the choice of music. I like listening to the wide range of music we had as kids before we got to our Brave New World. But the youngsters who operate TTM programs without even looking at the screens, say my enjoyment of chamber music composed centuries ago in old town Vienna just shows my age and how out-of-touch I am. I accept their judgement as I understand that, at my age, I probably do not fully appreciate all the benefits bestowed by the Krasnov Corporation.

ASSASSIN

"I think it is inevitable," Angie stated. She was one of my best students but tended to make extreme claims without noting the nuances of history. The History Faculty had only recently granted me a Professorship. I was not required to tutor undergraduates. My worth would be gauged by the volume of articles I could get published. But I enjoyed teaching and Angie was a joy.

"Tell me why you think political assassination must become more common."

Angie sat forward to emphasise her belief. I smiled as I could imagine her future as a political activist. She knows no fear in asserting what she believes to be true, irrespective of any counter arguments. Of course, as her tutor, my role is to present her with alternative views which should lead to a debate from which, hopefully, she could learn. I was almost looking forward to this but decided to refrain from confronting her until she had made her case.

"There has been a move towards leaders inventing political parties to support them rather than parties pushing through leaders from amongst their ranks. Look at Macron in France, Farage in the UK, and you might include the Republican Party in the USA being reinvented as the party of Trump. Opposition to these leaders' parties' policies is seen as opposition to the views of an individual leader. That's not the same as policies of a party that have evolved through discussion, debate and decision-making by many people. I think this is when the option of assassination becomes more attractive, even more rational."

"I see," I responded. "But who do you think would carry out such assassinations? It may appear to be more rational, but don't you think it can only become more common if there were some kind of organisation to make it practical, rather than just a passing thought."

"I think the possibility of success becomes more likely when the leader is balanced precariously above supporters who are merely followers with little grounding in policy formation."

"Can you give me some historical examples to support your theory? When have political assassinations been partially instigated, at least, by the victim being isolated at the top rather than a man or woman who has emerged from an active party?"

Angie stopped as she tried to think of examples that she had read about in preparing for the essay she had given me.

"Because of Trump, I started reading about assassinations of American Presidents."

"Well, you are not going to tell me that Abraham Lincoln was alone with his policies of retaining a union of States and the abolition of slavery, are you?"

"No, no. Of course not. But what about Garfield in 1881?"

"Ah! So, you think that Charles Guiteau, who believed he was acting alone on behalf of God, murdered Garfield to 'unite the Republican Party' as he put it?"

Angie frowned. "What about McKinley in 1901?"

"We could study the history of Anarchism in the years leading up to the First World War. Czolgosz was inspired by European anarchists who believed assassinations would help the poor by killing those who exploited them. But you could hardly argue that McKinley was a charismatic leader with his Republican Party merely following whatever he wanted. Like many ex-lawyers (even today), he was more a manager than a leader. I think it would be easier to argue that McKinley tended to follow the ideas generated from within the party."

"Kennedy in 1963 was the murder of a charismatic leader."

"True. But it would be hard to paint Lee Harvey Oswald as an assassin intent upon altering American policies by decapitating the man who he believed was spearheading those policies."

I knew that this could have led to an inconclusive dispute about who benefitted from John Kennedy's death: but Angie had an example up her sleeve about which I was ignorant.

"Olof Palme was assassinated in 1986. One theory about why he was targeted suggested that he was on the point of leading international condemnation and actions against the Iraqi government. They may have sent an assassin who successfully headed off anti-Iraqi action."

"Hmm. Interesting. I've not read that book. But that sounds like State-sponsored assassination. Perhaps the targeted killing of Palestinian leaders by Israeli forces is closer to that scenario. But, again, your thesis is that those Palestinian leaders, and Olof Palme in Sweden in the 1980s, had no groundswell of public support, as if they were the sole holder of views to which the public quietly succumbed. But that cannot be argued persuasively, surely."

I could see Angie was foundering but still suspected that her thesis could be argued. Her examples of Farage, Macron – and even Trump and the reconstituted Republican Party being structured in his image – could lead to the temptation to see assassination as a rational policy to decapitate the charismatic leader of a ragtag bunch of followers. It was time for me to introduce an element of learning that had been absent in Angie's essay and speech.

"Assassination was used as a powerful strategy against the Persian Seljuk Empire. Hasan-i- Sabbah conquered the fort of Alamut in 1090. Then, his agents took forts across Persia by targeted assassinations of military and political leaders – thus avoiding civilian casualties. A series of caliphs were assassinated by Nizari Ismaili followers of Hasan right through the eleventh and twelfth century."

"Ah yes, I've read about this!" Angie exclaimed. These ancient Assassins who believed there are very specific circumstances when they can justifiably kill those who are guilty of harm. They live by their set of rules, the Assassin's Creed."

"Really?" I smiled. "Tell me about that."

Angie became quite excited. "I read that in the ninth century, a man named Altaïr Ibn-La'Ahad codified the Assassin's creed. The creed was:

1. Stay your blade from the flesh of an innocent. That means that no innocent people could be killed – even as what we might call collateral damage – because the result would be against the interests of those for whom the assassination was carried out.

2. Hide in plain sight. This was central to the notion that the assassin was acting on behalf of the public amongst whom he could disappear once he had killed the target.

3. Never compromise the brotherhood. This meant that if captured or otherwise identified, the assassin would never admit to being part of the Brotherhood."

Angie was concentrating on remembering what she knew about this character. I decided to let her continue her flight of fancy.

"In 1191, in the struggle against the Knights Templars, Altaïr broke all three tenets by murdering an innocent, an old man whom he thought could have alerted guards. By revealing himself, Altaïr inevitably led the Templars back to the home of the Brotherhood, jeopardizing them all. Normally, this would have earned the death penalty, but instead, Altaïr was stripped of all his weapons and equipment, and demoted to the lowest rank of novice, and forced to re-earn his rank through assassinating nine select Templars."

"Sounds like the Mafia," I put in.

Angie looked very serious. "Yes, and as a secret organisation that may have existed for centuries before Altaïr, it certainly continued for many centuries afterwards. During the Renaissance, the Italian and Spanish Assassins recited a maxim at every new Assassin's induction into the Order. The maxim was: 'Nothing is true, everything is permitted.'"

"What does that mean?"

"In 1512, Ezio Auditore explained the maxim: To say that nothing is true is to realise that the foundations of society are fragile. Therefore, we are responsible for creating our own civilisation. To say that everything is permitted, is to understand that we are the architects of our actions, and that we must live with their consequences, whatever they may be.

In 1511, one of Ezio Auditore's Ottoman apprentices broke the first tenet after mistaking a cleric for the Templar Cyril of Rhodes and rashly assassinating him. Ezio ordered the apprentice to reflect on their mistake and to redeem himself when next confronting Cyril.

Ironically, Ezio himself indirectly broke the first tenet several times that year. He instigated a riot to gain access to a harbour, getting several civilians killed in the process. He rashly assassinated a Janissary captain whom he mistakenly believed was working with the Templars. But his biggest violation came in 1512, when he ignited the Templars' cache of gunpowder in Derinkuyu. The resulting firestorm killed many civilians. This made Ezio realise he was doing more harm than good, so he retired from the Order."

"So, do we still have the Order practising today?" I asked, somewhat mischievously.

Angie breezed on, recalling what she had read or heard.

"It was active in the 1790s during the Haitian and French revolutions. By then the belief was that the creed was an invocation commanding members not to see themselves as free, but instead to be wise. Around 1794, the French Assassin Arno Dorian explained that the maxim merely served as a guide and a warning, rather than a principle meant for an individual to follow. He had witnessed how ideals led to dangerous extremism. He is quoted as saying: Ideals too easily give way to dogma. Dogma becomes fanaticism. Only we can decide whether the road we walk carries too high a toll. All that we do, all that we are, begins and ends with ourselves."

I could not help chuckling but put on a serious face to comment. "So, this order of Assassins has a strict code. They intend to promote peace but commit murder. They appeal to people to reject oppressive regimes but require strict obedience to an ancient set of rules. And they reject society's tendency to unthinkingly obey laws and codes of conduct but expect blind faith in their own."

She replied instantly, like a true believer! "Absolutely! And true Assassins would instantly agree that their life is a constant process of living through inconsistencies and inevitable conflicts."

Despite Angie's wonderful reimagination of this well-known games series, I decided to continue to examine her thesis.

"So, if we are thinking about the likelihood of effective opposition to political leaders who appear to stand above and beyond their followers, we need to consider how such opposition would be carried out.

This would presumably be by some organised sect rather than by the odd individual acting alone, as in your American Presidential assassination examples."

She frowned and asked: "Has there been any more recent examples of an organised attempt on a despotic leader?"

"How about the army old guard, through men like Stauffenberg, attempting to assassinate Hitler on 20 July 1944? Many political commentators who advocate non-violence as a tenet of faith are uncomfortable when being asked to condemn Stauffenberg. What do you think, Angie? Do you think he was justified in trying to kill Hitler?"

"Absolutely. I would have no problem in supporting a man like that in such a situation."

I smiled. "So, if the Assassins were still active today, would you consider joining them?"

"I'm not sure about that. How would I even know if they were there if one of their rules was to hide in plain sight?"

"Perhaps your next essay could examine using non-fictional examples of how such despots or individual charismatics take power."

Angie nodded and stood up to leave. I remained seated peering over my desk furniture, a nightforce precision rifle scope

ARRESTED

Gordon was surprised when the officers arrived with an arrest warrant. "Subversion" was the only word he recognised when the warrant was flashed before his eyes. He was bundled into the van and driven to the police headquarters where he was placed on a hard, plastic chair behind a table. Two chairs on the other side of the table remained empty for ages. He wondered whether they had forgotten about him. Feeling cramped, he stood up. Instantly the door opened, and two officers entered. They sat down at the same moment. Their chairs scraped and Gordon's teeth were set on edge.

"Sit down!" one ordered.

Gordon carefully sat himself back and said: "why have you brought me here?". He was trying to imagine how they believed he was subversive. Maybe this was a case of mistaken identity. He waited to hear what they had to say.

One look at the other and commented, as if he was not there: "I wonder how long we'll have to wait until he tells us the truth."

Gordon decided he had better talk, even though nobody had asked him anything.

"Good morning, officers. I am happy to cooperate in anything you want me to take part in. Could you please give me a clue as to what I am meant to have done wrong?"

"We hardly need to tell you. You know very well what you've done."

"If I knew, I would be happy to talk about it. But please tell me what you want to ask me about."

"Listen, Mister Grant. We know that you've met with Julius James."

"Of course. I've known Julius for years. He was my doctor before he retired last year. But we've remained friends."

"When did you last see him?"

"Last week. We met to play our regular game of chess."

"Is that what you call it? A game of chess?"

"Yes. That is what we play. He is a better player than me: but I beat him last week. I think he wasn't concentrating."

"Really. So, what do you think he was concentrating on?"

Gordon shrugged. "Not sure. Maybe he was worrying about what to cook for dinner. He has been trying to follow a strict diet: but not very well, I believe."

The two officers looked at one another. After about half a minute's ominous silence one of them opened a folder and seemed to be reading a sheet of paper. Then he turned to Gordon and said: "That is not all you met him for, was it? We know that you talked about the dangers faced by our political leaders."

Gordon frowned, trying to recall all the chitchat that had been thrown up between friends. Then he thought long and hard about how these two men knew about a private conversation. Was Julius' room bugged? Had Julius talked to someone about what had been said? Finally, he tried to recall what remarks he may have made about current politics.

"Please remind me, if you would. What am I supposed to have said? I honestly cannot remember exactly what we talked about."

The interviewer read from his sheet of paper. "I would not be surprised if someone tried to assassinate him. Those were your words. Do you remember now?"

Gordon Grant paused. Where was this leading? He was scarcely the most probable assassin suspect – an eighty-year-old with a dicky heart, short-sighted and quite sad after his wife of sixty years had died six months earlier. He decided to try to reason with the officers.

"I honestly do not recall saying those words but, like you no doubt, I am aware that there has been a great deal more political violence internationally. My concern, which I am sure that you share, is that these troubled times could mean greater threats to our elected leaders. I may have been sharing these worries with my old friend who also knows that violence is no answer to resolving disputes".

The two looked at one another. One shook his head whilst the other replaced the paper in the folder. It seemed to Gordon that either he would be told to go now, or he would be charged with something like sedition for daring to suggest to his chess partner that assassination was more likely in an era of political violence. Surely, he argued with himself, these two cannot honestly believe that I am some sort of marksman with sights set on our president! That would be absurd.

"How did you imagine assassination might be carried out?" one asked him.

"I have no idea. I suppose, as guns are so easy to acquire in our country, shooting is the most common danger."

"And you are saying you know nothing about the attempt that was about to be made?!"

"What! Someone has tried to shoot the president! I don't believe it. That would have been on the news."

"Some things are not on the news, but those involved know all about it before it takes place, don't they?"

"Hang on. Are you saying that some madman has tried to shoot the president and that I am, in some way, in collusion with whoever this man or woman is. And Julius and I are some sort of clandestine assassination squad? That's crazy! How on earth could you believe that?"

"We have had Julius under observation for a long time and the conversations that he has with you are more suspicious than anything else we have in our networked anti-conspiracy team's observations. We believe that you have sanctioned and recruited potential assassins."

"What rubbish! Who are we meant to have recruited? Who are our assassins?"

"Julius's son is a prime suspect."

"Vincent James! An assassin! How do you reckon that?"

"We know he was in the capital at the same time as the president and we know that he always travels armed."

"You're talking about Bishop Vincent James who was attacked by thugs last year and, under advice from the police, carries a derringer to deter any future threats."

"That's the man! And we heard you say to Julius James … and here I quote you word for word

… "the bishop will be a serious threat to the king."

Do you deny saying that?"

Gordon opened his mouth but repressed a laugh. "I was talking about the chess game."

"Yes. Of course you were. Next you will be telling us that the assassination attempt on the president had nothing to do with Vincent James."

"So, what are you saying? Vincent raised himself out of his wheelchair. Then somehow shot the President with a derringer. This is ridiculous."

"We believe Vincent must have more powerful weapons than a derringer."

"Well, why don't you arrest him and charge him?"

The officers looked at one another. Then one said: "Are you saying you know nothing about the bishop firing at the President?"

"I have no idea what you are talking about. The notion that Biship Vincent is some sort of deranged killer – this is the invention of a crazy conspiracy theorist. Where did you get such an insane idea? From comments Julius and I make about our chess games?"

"Don't play the innocent with us!" one shouted.

"How can I do anything other than appear innocent? I've done nothing wrong."

"How do you explain the attempt on the president this morning?"

"What?! Is he OK? Killing him would be to no purpose, even if you disagree with him."

"Ah! So, you admit to disagreeing with him!"

"My political opinions are irrelevant. I knew nothing about any attempt on the life of the president and I sincerely doubt that Julius's disabled son is in any way involved. Now, unless you want to charge me with something, I insist that you let me go or let me call a lawyer to help me get home as soon as possible."

"The attempt was made two hours ago. The location, as we believe you know, was in the private chapel used by the president and to which Bishop Vincent has access. We cannot identify who was in the chapel at the time other than the security guards. But that does not mean that Vincent was not present. The news blackout has been complete because we do not want to cause panic. We are holding you here until we can prove your involvement with the president's assassination."

"You mean he is dead!"

"You already know this and now Vincent has been in touch with Julius."

"You mean Julius's son has phoned his dad. What is that meant to prove?"

"We don't know yet. But we'll know all about it soon as we've unscrambled what we recorded on their tapped phones. The words we could make out on the crackly line talked about the bishop's declaration: listen to this: "…Father …thy kingdom…come on earth … deliver us from evil…""

"That's bits of the Lord's prayer."

"We know that. But why would he be citing that to his father?

"You are asking why a bishop is citing the Lord's Prayer?"

"This is a code to report a successful assassination."

"Are you telling me that President is dead?"

"You know this already!"

"How could I possibly know this?"

"You are part of the assassination squad. We have arrested Julius now. When we find Vincent, he will join us. Do you know where he will be?"

"Probably in the cathedral citing the Lord's Prayer!"

One of the officers rushed out. He returned a minute later.

"How did you know he would be in the cathedral?"

"I didn't know. But he is the bishop, and that is his place of work.

--

The news headlines the next day reported that the assassination had been carried out by powerful, evil forces and the suspects were under arrest.

GRENDON

One may as well hang for a sheep as a lamb

Grendon was the strangest creature Joseph had ever come across. Extraterrestrial beings often visited the planet but usually kept their distance. Joseph was well known for having claimed contact with many of them. But most regarded him as an eccentric dreamer and took little notice of his occasional claims

"Honestly, I've met many of them," he told the local tv journalist sent to do an amusing feature on a man about whom viewers could have a little giggle at the end of the local news. But Grendon appeared one night in a flurry of wind and sand. Joseph was not perturbed by the stranger's arrival. None had ever harmed him, and some had spoken in his own language with scarcely a hint of foreign accent.

"Why do you want to speak to me?" he asked.

Grendon did not speak. It communicated in a way that he had never experienced. It was as if it was talking from inside his own head.

"I have been watching you. You are a creature that other humans seem to regard with suspicion. Why do they believe that you are plotting against others? Do you know why that is the case?"

Joseph had to think about this question. At first, he

wondered if Grendon was referring to the article lampooning his claims of meeting non-terrestrial beings. But mention of plotting reminded him of strange people who seemed to think he was within a vast network of conspirators wanting to take control of the planet.

"You must mean the idiots who believe that there is a secret society that plans to seize power. I have no idea why people hold these irrational beliefs. I assume it is because these are ideas fed to them by genuinely powerful people who want to deflect attention from their own positions of power."

Grendon seemed to swirl upwards like a tiny tornado before settling back like a cloud on the ground. Grendon appeared to grumble before asking: "What would you do if you had the power that these conspiracy theorists believe you have?"

Joseph scratched his head. When he was much younger, he had studied history in a famous University that introduced him to an infamous tract entitled 'The Protocols of the Elders of Zion." He remembered how it had been used to build upon centuries of anti-Semitism to reinforce the idea that Jews like him somehow met in secret to take control of the World. He spoke disdainfully to Grendon.

"People who believe they can somehow make the world better by seizing power always seem to end up as worse than those they are determined to replace."

Grendon seemed to laugh – it was a horrible gurgle that rose up from inside him. It made him feel slightly nauseous. Grendon recognised this instantly and apologised. "Sorry about that. I dd not mean to make you feel ill. I simply wondered whether you have much to lose."

"What do you mean?"

"I think you have a saying "one may as well hang for a sheep as a lamb". You already have all the disadvantages of being distrusted as a secret plotter but without any of the advantages of controlling through this non-existent conspiracy. So, how would you feel if you were granted these powers?

Joseph smirked. "Then all the suspicions of the idiotic conspiracy theorists would be proved correct!"

Grendon seemed to roll around on the ground. Joseph frowned as he watched this display.

"Grendon, are you laughing?"

"I was enjoying the irony. But I still want to know your answer."

Joseph scratched his head. "What on earth would you do? Are you saying you could accomplish deeds impossible for we humans?"

"Not really. Grendon can destroy but not construct. If you want anything positive, you'll have to do that yourself. But I can dispose of all those conspiracy theorists and evil men who hold power in your nations.”

“You mean you can kill people at my bidding?”

“Yes”

“But that would leave me no better than the awful men you would be murdering.”

“Well, it would not really seem like murder. Everyone would think it was natural causes, or old age, or an unfortunate infection. No one would suspect you.”

Joseph thought about this. He certainly felt tempted. The list of dictators inflicting pain and death upon thousands of people did not strike him as men who deserved to survive. If this Grendon could quietly dispose of these disgusting examples of humanity, Joseph could not see that anything worse would be the result. On the other hand, the people who put these creatures in charge of their countries would probably simply replace one devil with another. And Jospeh himself would have done nothing other than confirm the worst suspicions of the crazy conspiracy theorists.

Grendon read all Joseph’s thoughts. Rising slowly into the sky, Grendon left Jospeh with a parting thought. “Very well, you are a good and thoughtful man. I shall leave you now and will not return.”

Grendon seemed to dissipate like a cloud of smoke. Joseph breathed a sigh of relief. He did not enjoy the dilemmas presented by beings like Grendon. He never knew what the right answer was.

The next day, the newspapers were full of the unexpected news of the death of the leaders of two of the most powerful nations. The following days saw similar news from other nations. Some thought it was the result of a new pandemic that only seemed to affect older, over-powerful males. Some attributed it to a shadowy secret society with invisible tentacles that reached into the darkest reaches of the best protected citadels guarding men against all-comers day and night. Joseph decided that he would keep his conscience clean by writing about Grendon in a short story that, despite being read by millions, was written off as the fantasy of an elderly science fiction writer.

HYDRA

Iolaus slept fitfully. He was the best golf caddy on the tour. He had been offered large bribes to defect from his longtime friend and partner and join those of richer teams. But the celebrity Golf club President, nicknamed Mr. Putt, had a bombastic style that riled the peaceful Iolaus: and the other wealthy team of Mr. Putting (a close friend of Mr. Putt) was known for underhand tactics – even descending to harming opponents.

Iolaus was haunted by nightmares. He imagined striding across the links, carrying a fine set of clubs, accompanied by uniformed members of the Putt or Putting team who were following their leaders. Suddenly, these opposing caddies and supporters turned on him demanding that he hand over his clubs. One moment they all seemed to be happily playing the game; but the next moment the rules and traditional courtesies of golf were thrown over, replaced by mob rule as Iolaus was alone facing these thugs.

The morning saw Iolaus sickened by the content of his dream. He had awakened before handing over the clubs but could see no alternative to caving in to the demands of the Putt and Putting bully boys. He washed and dressed, then carefully checked the clubs he had cleaned the night before to be ready for the match starting in the afternoon. He saw no advantage in telling his top-ranked leader about the nightmare. Instead, he encouraged him to use the drivers even when irons might normally have been used because he had carefully analysed the strengths of his play on this course. There was a good reason why he was regarded as the best caddy. Sure enough, at those critical moments when Iolaus's advice was heeded, the match was won

Mr. Putt claimed that the game had been stolen from him and Putting agreed. But it was not until the following year that the competition found Putt winning with support from Putting's men. They distracted Iolaus and his leader with nocturnal noises preventing restful sleep in the nights before the match. Nothing could be proved so Mr. Putt took the prize trophy.

Iolaus learnt that Mr. Putt intended to keep the trophy and not hand it back for the following year's competition. Putt and Putting were actively pressing the tournament organisers to abandon any future competition being played. Instead, they have bought and handed over the rights to the competition to a billionaire who is busily persuading young competitors to play golf online on a platform that he owns.

Iolaus is now enduring a recurring dream. The world's golf courses have been turned into vast shopping malls. His golfing superstar is wielding a number five iron that transforms into an executioner's axe as it is brought down upon the necks of the caddies and supporters of

Putt and Putting. Iolaus follows with a burning torch to cauterise the beheaded opponents to prevent them growing new heads. The five iron is dropped in favour of the number two driver as Mr. Putt and Putting confront them. The dream ends with the mythical superstar dispatching the heads of the two gangster crime bosses with the driver supplied by Iolaus

CHEVAUCHÉE

"Listen, my son," the General, was speaking. I attended closely because he became angry if I failed to take in all he said. At the Military Academy, he was known for his short temper. As a father he was always attentive to my needs as a child. But now, having reached the mature age of thirteen, he regarded me as an adult. He was away shouting orders at the Academy recruits on parade when my mother asked me what I wanted to do when I grew up. I whispered I would like to learn to play the piano and become a musician. She advised me strongly to keep this ambition to myself. "Your father might not like to hear that."

The General came home and took me aside. I was embarrassed because I was anticipating an awful session where he thought he was doing every father's duty – to explain the reproductive process and the necessity of using contraceptives during sexual intercourse. I dreaded this as he would undoubtedly stray into declaring homosexuality a perversion that he would not tolerate in any child of his. At thirteen, I had little idea about my sexuality as I had not had any opportunity to try it out. Although I was probably not a homosexual, I could see no reason to regard any friend who thought he was as less of a friend.

"Now listen, my son," I was already groaning inwardly. "There are certain things that every young man needs to know. It took me some years to realise how important what I am about to divulge to you will be for your life. Although you will have many years before you to practise what is, at your age, just theory. It is never too early to be introduced to these critical facts of life."

I was starting to get bored; but had to restrain myself. Implying how ridiculous this speech was would have been seen as a gross display of indiscipline. But he was pausing and looking to me, as if awaiting some show of attendance.

"Yes, sir." I nodded as if encouraging him to carry on.

"Very well," he continued as he turned to his desk. I started to shiver with horror. 'Oh my God!' I thought to myself. 'I do hope he is not about to open his drawer and reveal a display of condoms and other apparatus associated with sex.' I was starting to sweat and blush. I took out my handkerchief as if to blow my nose: it was just an excuse to cover my mouth and face to hide whatever involuntary expressions he might cause.

"Right. I want no excuses. There is nothing more important than Sun Tzu's 'The Art of War' and Machiavelli's 'The Prince'. They are essential reading." And he placed the books on the desk for me to take. I took a sharp intake of breath: I have no idea if this was shock or relief. But he took it to be a good sign.

"I am glad to see how excited you feel about being introduced to these two masters. As a young man, you will find them essential reading in everything you do and, especially, when you are older and take command of troops."

I decided there and then to go along with the General's wish. After all, what harm could there be in reading a couple of books? Mother was clearly unimpressed: I think she was hoping that I would improve myself by reading classic literature. But, for the sake of peace with the General, I read both Machiavelli's and Sun Tzu's famous works. He told mother he was delighted to find me reading Sun Tzu – an author whom he regarded as superior to such a poor player as William Shakespeare or a weak peacenik like Leo Tolstoy. Then, to cap it all, he was appointed as Director of the Military Academy! My ambition to become a professional musician looked more distant than ever as we went to live in the grounds of the Academy – surrounded by recruits more intent upon keeping khaki clean than pursuing perfection through patient piano practice.

Mother knew I was unhappy but felt unable to support my ambition. For her, being the Academy Director's wife gave her all the status she craved. How her son coped with his musical dreams against the reality of family life was up to him to resolve. It is ironic how the solution to my dilemma was presented through a profound understanding of the teaching of my father's author heroes.

The one interest I shared with the Academy recruits was the latest electronic wargames. The earliest had leaned heavily upon spectacular graphics and the challenge of speedy responses to 'enemy' appearances on screen. But with the dawn of the avatar-based games where the player imagined himself to be at one with his selected avatar on screen, a new fantasy life was being presented. The addictive qualities of the latest games were bound to affect students. Loss of attention to detail, a sharp decline in interest in their chosen area of study and the sheer amount of screen time craved and taken led to major problems for those in charge of educational institutions. It was me who deliberately introduced the latest game to the new recruits. Soon they all were playing the appropriately named Chevauchée. (A term commonly used in the 100 Years War but with startlingly new appeal to contemporary warmongers).

The General was defeated by one of the oldest strategies: the diversionary attack aimed at the demoralisation of his army. By the time he had learnt to co-exist with his defeated, distracted student cohort, he had ceased attending to his wayward son.

My pianist career began with a shelf of Beethoven sonatas and Chopin studies alongside the texts of Machiavelli and Sun Tzu.

GLINE

It seems that the Glines have been observing Earth for longer than humans have been around. Their interest in our planet only grew for one reason. According to the top military minds of our generation, this could only have been because of our development of Caesar Rays that could destroy entire armies from cunningly positioned satellite gunships. But when Lobin, whom our enemies labelled a "gung-ho dictator", decided to turn Caesar Rays towards the galactic cloud apparently housing Gline positions, he learnt to his and our cost that it was not this that interested them. The Ray's instant deflection back to its source decimated much of the military establishment that had been lovingly grown by our esteemed leader.

The destruction was blamed upon homegrown saboteurs, but we all know it was the Glines who had decided to teach us a lesson. The way that Gline contact had been established should have given a clue to the focus of their interest. When the complex patterns of signals were picked up, there were numerous attempts to decipher their meaning. The men and women tasked with decoding reported a feeling of warmth and affection pervading the otherwise clinically cold, hygienic laboratories in which they worked. Their decoding computer units trembled as they extracted snatches of linguistic output: but most decoding machines hummed and emitted what sounded like birdsong rather than intelligible words. It was the Gline's apparent ignoring our attempts to communicate verbally which made Lobin and others like him infer that Glines had ill intentions that they were hiding through silence or gibberish.

After the elimination of Lobin's capacity to wage Caesar Ray war, no other nation followed his lead. An Australian team broadcast into space a wide variety of pictorial imagery from ancient aboriginal cave paintings to ultra-modern conceptual creations. They were rewarded by non-visual responses, but the wave patterns seemed to make the building where they worked vibrate. It was not until a Chinese team played a recording of a traditional folk song accompanied by a virtuoso guzheng player that the Gline response came back with an astonishing display of orchestral sound — but with instrumentation unlike anything that we used on Earth. The Chinese team shared the recording with other astronomy teams around the world and their collective opinion was that Gline culture had evolved to communicate through music.

"Perhaps they will like our latest pop songs and dance music" media outlets proclaimed who, also, happened to own the rights to play and distribute these mass-produced items. But Gline response to having this blasted out through space was muted. As the Chinese folk song had stimulated a response, other folk melodies from around the world were tried but with only limited success. Eventually, the virtuoso performance on the guzheng was identified as being the focus of their interest. And so it proved as recordings by the top pianists and violinists performing recognised masterpieces brought forth an avalanche of Gline soundscapes that matched the virtuosity of the world's greatest players.

Without any apparent linguistic communication system, our cleverest analysts were at a loss as to how Gline civilisation had evolved. Their technology appeared to be so many centuries more advanced than Earth's that we were unable to understand answers to the most fundamental questions we asked. How do you travel around the Universe? How do you procreate? Even, "what does a Gline look like?"

After a couple of months, the screen on an American astronomer's desk flickered into life – even though he had not turned it on. There was an image whose authenticity many have since questioned. "This must be a trick. Why do Americans always think they have to lead on major breakthroughs? We don't believe any of it." These were standard responses around the rest of the world, but the image looked like a female human being, albeit one with almost superhuman characteristics. She spoke in perfect English and explained that Gline interest had been sparked by some of the latest recordings of music by Bach, Mozart, Beethoven, Prokofiev, and Olivier Messiaen. Other composers were of intense interest, but Gline musical leadership had identified four or five specific recordings that they valued. Then she explained that Gline individuals communicate with one another through musical imagery. "We find this to be far more comprehensive in setting out how and why we think or feel rather than the ancient system that we used to use that you call spoken language."

The astonished astronomer had asked the name of the female addressing them. What sounded like human laughter was accompanied by an explanation that there was no female speaking to them, only an image that the Gline had created together with an attempt to communicate in a clumsy foreign language so that humans could try to grasp a little about Gline culture. "What do you really look like?" was met with a blank screen.

Lobin's response to Gline's apparent love of fine music was to have scores of leading performers and composers imprisoned. They were tried in courts whose judges had been appointed by Lobin. They were accused of being in secret communication with Glines using music that Lobin had decided should be banned.

Their guilt was decided prior to their appearance in court. To emphasise the message, Lobin had a concert grand piano ceremonially destroyed with axes and televised on the evening news. The piano was declared to have been the secret communication medium used to send messages to the Glines. Some of Lobin's henchmen whose military hardware had been destroyed when they had attempted to Caesar Ray the Glines took it upon themselves to hunt down musicians and music teachers. One old lady who had taught the piano to preschool children died when Lobin's mob broke into her house.

Opponents of Lobin who had fled abroad appealed for help. But he had provided no pretext for others to intervene in the internal running of the country. Funds were raised to support the families of imprisoned musicians although it is doubtful that much actually got through to the intended recipients. Music composed in support of 'Rebels Against Lobin' (R.A.L.) filled the airways and was fed through the Internet to keep up the spirits of those committed to R.A.L.. But Lobin had much social media shut down and foreign radio and tv stations had their signals jammed. The Caesar Ray catastrophe had taught him to focus his violent attention only upon human adversaries.

Gline intervention arrived in ways that Lobin found difficult to contain. In response to a German broadcast with outstanding performers playing famous concertos for violin and orchestra, the Gline responded with what we now believe was their version of a concert. It was received by radio stations on every continent, and, despite Lobin's best efforts, nothing could prevent their music being heard by anyone with a radio. The seriously catchy tune that concluded the Gline performance was whistled and sung by children in every country – including ours and there seemed that Lobin could do nothing about it.

R.A.L. even set revolutionary words to the theme and it became their anthem. Lobin gave orders that anyone singing it in public should be shot.

There was huge controversy over the circumstances surrounding the death of our leader. Lobin made many enemies and being human, of course he made mistakes. But he achieved a level of economic growth that benefitted much of our population and gained the unswerving support of our religious authorities who claimed he was a "true patriot". In elections, he usually won by taking over ninety nine percent of the votes – an astonishing achievement unequalled anywhere else in the world. Enemies abroad claimed he ran a corrupt dictatorship – but he said that they were just envious of his achievements. There was no one with him when he died so there were no witnesses to what happened. When his personal assistant arrived in the morning, the house servants opened the door and let him go up the stairs to present Lobin with documents that needed his signature. As there was no response to his request to enter the private apartment, the head butler was called to open the door with his electronic key. On entering, they found Lobin dead, in bed, wearing earphones playing live music.

Despite opposition from the military authorities, most of our imprisoned musicians have now been released. Intriguingly, the generals in charge of the army were persuaded to take no action against even the most rebellious musicians by their own military band members. R.A.L. disbanded and the forthcoming election looks as if the party containing the most hardline religious leaders may not have enough support to gain more than just a couple of seats in our parliament. The leader of the most popular party, and the one that has garnered massive support from well-wishers around the world, is a celebrated clarinettist who used to perform in the city's jazz clubs before being imprisoned by our late leader. The one great disappointment since Lobin's strange death has been the absolute silence from the Glines as if they are no longer there.

THE DINNER PARTY

John and Sue invited Sandra and I to dinner, together with their friends Fred and Francis. We had all known each other for many years. We all felt we could say anything here: no one would take offense from such close friends.

So, I was surprised by the uncomfortable silence that followed when I asked if anyone had seen the old fellow who pushed his trolley around the local roads.

"I've not seen him recently. Perhaps something has happened," I said

"Has he had an accident?" Sandra asked.

"No. I saw him yesterday," Sue announced. "He was pushing his trolley around the field behind the shops."

"He seems pretty harmless," Francis added. "He must be well into his seventies."

"I doubt that." Fred intervened. "I've seen him running with his trolley. He must be in his forties… maybe fifties."

"He spoke to me once," Sandra said.

"What did he say to you?" I was curious about what he would have said to my wife.

"He asked me about our kids."

"I asked him about his trolley once," Francis piped up. We all looked at her to discover what she had discovered about his mysterious perambulator that had been stripped down to leave very little beyond a simple, covered box on wheels.

"What did he say? We all asked at once.

Francis was quite taken aback by hearing five of us all demanding to know what words had been spoken to her by a relative stranger.

"Wait a minute, let me think." She frowned trying to recall his words. I was beginning to wish I had not asked about this man. After all, I was not especially interested in what this rag-and-bone lookalike was pushing around in his makeshift cart.

"I think he was trying to crack a joke. He said he always kept his liquor store with him so that if he felt depressed, he could go home legless!"

Fred was unamused. "Perhaps he thought that was funny."

We sat reflecting on this for a moment.

"Do you think he may have had some sort of breakdown?" I asked.

"I think that's quite likely," John replied. "I had a conversation with him over a year ago. He seemed obsessed with some theory about how our society functions. I didn't understand many of the words he used: I think he must have been some sort of lecturer, once upon a time."

"Do you remember anything he said?" Fred asked.

"I think he may have been a musician who had made

recordings of his music because he said he kept listening to some of his compositions from years ago, just to remember how things used to be."

"Oh! Isn't that sweet?" Sandra exclaimed. "Did he say anything else?" I asked, risking the conversation becoming boring through too much persistence. But John continued, "he talked about how he thought our society had deteriorated. He thought musicians would run the country much better."

"He sounds like a lunatic wandering around the country declaring that God is dead," Fred said. "Is he one of those old-timers always looking back to some non-existent golden age?"

"Probably. But he was quite well-versed in all sorts of things to do with politics and economics that I found difficult to follow," John admitted.

"A musical political scientist! How unusual" Francis commented.

"He seemed sad," John concluded.

"Why?" I asked, risking the looks of impatience from those who wanted the conversation to pass on to more interesting subjects.

"He said that just as some who have lost limbs continue to feel them as if they are really there, we continue to believe we live in a liberal democracy although, in reality, we now live with ghost limbs that have been surgically removed."

The evening ended and we complimented Sue on the delightful dinner she had prepared. Then, we laughed at the ritual comedy of deciding the order in which our six amputee wheelchairs could exit the room.

ANGELIC HOST

It is extremely annoying when you go in for a service and the job is not carried out. Despite protestations to the contrary that the work had been completed to the required standard, actions speak louder than words.

I have flown for enough years to know if a wing has been properly mended. I was carrying out a quick tour when I came down with a bump. The woman I nearly knocked over screamed and within a minute she had half a dozen men running to her assistance. I tried to explain that my landing was an accident, but she would not listen. She kept shouting and pointing to my shoulder where the damaged wing was protruding.

It was abundantly clear to me that unless I acted promptly, it would be more than my wing that was torn. I had never used the time transformation facility, but this was an emergency. The mob seemed to me to have frozen in time although I knew that this was just an illusion. Brushing past the men I was tempted to give the meanest looking one a punch on the nose, but I thought better of it and just ran on leaving them perplexed as to how the stranger had disappeared.

My priority was to get the wing mended. But I was unsure how to go about this without even knowing where I had landed. The countryside around here was green and peaceful but devoid of passers-by who might have been able to show me where I could get at least a temporary fix.

On the hill at the top of the road, there was a large poster board. Perhaps that might give me a clue as to where I should go. I walked slowly up the hill, annoyed at not being able to flit through the air as usual. By the time I had reached the top, I was feeling tired and out-of-breath. Perhaps my condition, combined with the aggravation caused by the useless engineering crew to whom I am attached for wing maintenance, explained my non-angelic reaction to what I saw.

The picture of the man demanding my vote at the forthcoming presidential election in no way resembled those we had been shown at angel school in the lessons about dictators responsible for the death of millions. However, there was something about his demeanour that told me that he would soon join them in our next seminar as a more up-to-date example. I was so angry just at the sight of his smug face that I fired a tiny posterior thunderbolt that destroyed the posterboard in a flash.

I looked around to see if anyone had witnessed this unforgiveable act of vandalism. We were taught the importance of non-interference from our very first days at school. We are told that humans are responsible for their own fates. The contrary opinion held by the 'cetacean team' whom I must admit I respected although, clearly, they did not have sanctification from on high, was that we should intervene for the sake of the truly innocent. They had a three-dimensional image of Moby Dick that they projected onto the wall whenever we had this discussion. Their belief was that the only creatures that held value in these terms were whales. Therefore, intervention on their behalf was an angelic duty. The problem that they had in arguments at school was that once intervention was seen as permissible in one case; others were sure to follow. So, our teachers explained that this was the 'slippery slope' doctrine which officially ruled out intervention and the very highest authority proclaimed that it would never be sanctioned.

I was pondering about this old argument as I walked down the hill. I know I have an unfortunate habit of talking to myself. "Stop mumbling!" I was told throughout my childhood, but it is difficult to prevent yourself doing something that is part of your very makeup.

"Perhaps the will to intervene is itself part of some angels' makeup," I said to myself.

"What did you say?"

I was startled by this voice. A woman on a bicycle had been riding down the hill and came alongside me just as I was muttering.

"Oh. Sorry. I didn't see you. I was just talking to

myself."

"Did you see the posterboard? Someone has a real attitude daring to destroy one of his posters. If any of his supporters saw the culprit, they would beat him up like they've done to other opponents in the city. It wasn't you, was it?" she asked coyly. She knew very well it was me, but I thought it would be amusing to play innocent.

"Why? Are you going to beat me up," I replied.

She laughed. "Look back up there. You'll see that I followed up your demolition by setting fire to the wreckage. My friends and I would do anything to see that vile man beaten in the election. But we know that will never happen as he always wins. He has those mad supporters who thinks he is some kind of god – and that includes powerful people who run the media here."

I nodded as if I knew what she was talking "You aren't from around here, are you?" she said.

"No. Actually, you might be able to help me. I'm looking for someone who can do some running repairs."

"What sort of repairs?"

"If I had an injured pet. Where would I go if it were a bird with a damaged wing?"

"You would need a vet. And guess what? I am a veterinary surgeon with my own practice. So, if you show me your bird, I am sure I can help."

I looked at the young woman. Could I trust her with the sight of my wing? She would know that I was certainly not from "around here". But, there again, what choice did I have? Perhaps I could erase some part of her memory. I had heard that some colleagues had achieved this, but I had never tried it. With no one else in sight, I pulled off my overall and revealed my injury.

"Well, I never!" she exclaimed. "So, you are the pet!" and she burst out laughing. Eventually, she calmed down and started a professional inspection of my wing.

"I can sort this out," she announced. "But I want you to do something for me as payment."

"Sorry. I have no money."

"I don't want money. I want you to do something instead."

"How quick can you repair the wing?"

She reached into her saddlebag and pulled out what looked like a long comb. "Stand still," she demanded. I waited for her to hold me by my shoulder, but she went straight for the wing with her comb. After a minute of feather combing, the wing suddenly jumped by itself, then settled down into its natural position."

"That should work," she said. "You'll find it will function fine now."

I extended both wings and found take-off very easy. A quick circle around and I returned beside my saviour.

"I want to thank you very much. Tell me what I can

do for you."

"You know the man whose picture you destroyed. I want you to somehow discover what horrible things he is planning so we can prepare our defences."

I wondered whether this would break the non-interference rule. If this politician had no notion of who I was and never learnt how his enemies discovered his secrets, I couldn't see how I could be admonished as it would all seem to happen as if I'd not been there.

"Where will I find him? And how will I find you afterwards?"

The vet cyclist pulled out a notepad from her bag and scribbled instructions for me.

"I trust you to carry out what you promised," she said as I took off on my way to where she had instructed me to fly.

The capital was easy to find. Smoke and exhaust fumes filled the atmosphere for hundreds of kilometres in all directions. I surveyed the city and quickly identified where the leader was installed. It seems that the more odious the leader, the more layers of physical protection are built around him. I landed on a balcony that I calculated would bring me near what they call "the seat of power" (I never understood what a chair had to do with power). Pushing open the bay window I found myself in an empty room with a large table upon which were several heavily marked maps. Curious, I started studying them.

Suddenly, the door at the other end of the room opened and half a dozen men marched in accompanied by the leader. They could not see me as I had used an aspect of the time transformation facility that made their perception of me impossible without angelic spectacles. The men were pointing at the maps, and the leader was shouting about how they needed to be more precise about where the attacks should be aimed.

"Through the sea," one replied. And the others all nodded in agreement.

"How many of our men would die?" another asked

. The leader scowled at him as if it was an irrelevant question.

"The explosions offshore when the fighting begins will bring us lots of fish floating to our table," one laughed.

It was only at that moment that I realised the men were being watched by the entire cetacean team – all wearing angelic spectacles and looking straight at me!

"What are you doing here?" one asked me.

"Never mind me: what are you lot doing

"Today, we are the angelic host!"

"So, are you here to stop me interfering?

"Stop questioning and answer us."

"I promised to report this man's plans to his opponents. But otherwise, I won't interfere. Why?

What are you doing here?"

"You can go and do your report," the team leader replied, "and you can tell them that the heart attack that is about to kill this leader has been ordered by Moby Dick."

An image of the giant whale flashed up onto the wall behind the leader. All his people saw it just as their boss clasped his chest and collapsed. The image disappeared and so did the cetacean team.

It only took me five minutes to fly to where my vet saviour had cycled home. I told her that the leader's death, which would be reported next day, had nothing to do with me. She smiled, nodded, but clearly did not believe me. Unfortunately, no one up here believes me either, because the cetacean team deny all knowledge of what happened. On the other hand, the repair to my shoulder by a woman who was a major opponent of the dead leader is well recorded.

This has now set me up as the prime suspect in the upcoming anti-interference trial. I've even had my wings clipped! The useless wing engineering team have a lot to answer for.

OUROBOROS

This is the story of Leo. At least, that is how I knew him mostly. Others have told me that his gender was uncertain and that some knew him as Leonie when he dressed as a woman. However, I have never considered this an issue of interest although others have tried to assert that this was a critical factor in Leo's life and the decisions and discoveries that are attributed to him.

Leo's father, Xavier, was a celebrated cleric. Whether he was a leading Islamic scholar or Christian teacher is a matter of debate. Categorising him into these religious pigeonholes seems to me to be of purely academic interest. His impact upon philosophical theory, as well as his influence over Leo, does not require an easy placement within established schools of thought. I have always found his followers' desperate grasp of his best-known aphorism rarely follows a further understanding of its meaning. 'Without water, there could be no tree, and without tree, there could be no crucifixion' seems to have been best understood by Leo.

Xavier was working in the era of the Autocrats. This was not his choice: he just happened to have been born in the wealthiest nation where it was considered heretical to poke fun at the political leadership. I was in the audience when the most controversial film show was raided by the police, and I found myself in a cell for a couple of days with Leo. The film 'MAGA' was a remake of the old 'Planet of the Apes' movie where the oppressive, armed enforcers were called the 'Monkeys And Gorillas Authority' – much to the chagrin of the actual President. The filmmaker was my talented twin sister, Artemis. But it was the record of Leo's attendance at this show which, later, influenced critical decisions about his true political allegiances.

I will admit that my own feelings regarding patriotism are ambiguous. Like everyone else whom we knew at college and beyond, it was the ideals of democracy, liberty, social equality, and other principles of the Enlightenment to which we aspired. However, as there seemed to be nowhere in this world where these ideals were practised, alternative commitments were made to survive in the actual world in which we lived. Artemis was hounded out of the country and went to live in Norway. My exile from MAGA land is of marginal importance to the story of Leo: but his deportation to the other great Autocracy was a critical moment in this century's evolution.

My work as an image recognition scientist was of minor significance, but the projects upon which I and hundreds of others worked were important. Leo's saw the development of 'merones' as a logical follow through from understanding Xavier's saying. The conceptualisation of what I naively thought of as deep structures that pervaded the Universe which could be accessed even at molecular level was what Leo explained lay behind his father's thinking. Xavier wrote about these universal structures (he regarded the Cross as one) rather like Jung wrote about archetypes that pervade the dream world of people from differing cultures. Each of us casts our own image structures onto the molecular environment within which we live. The manipulation of what we cast by invading this personal space offered an entirely new set of weaponry. 'Merones' (an abbreviation of Molecular Drones) offered a tempting means by which to influence or even assassinate an opponent.

The initial attempts to assassinate President Zed using comparatively crude MAGA merones merely led to the rapid detention of those who had tried flooding the environment with thousands of merones in the hope that one or two would penetrate the defence dome. Zed, in retaliation, tasked his brother Gregory with developing far more powerful merones for a MAGA assault. The laboratory where I was working became a hive of activity attempting to reinforce the dome shields as the race to develop the best defences became a priority for autocrats on every continent.

Whether it was with or without the permission of his brother, Gregory decided to use merones upon those he regarded as political opponents within the country.

He would build various dome structures around them and, if they did not work, he simply reported their death to a grateful President Zed. But Gregory was not as adept as the MAGA technicians in creating the most lethal merones, nor how to stop them. Some whispered rumours in our laboratories suggested that perhaps Gregory was not averse to the possibility of Zed succumbing to the next attack, leaving the leadership open for him. The prospect of a Gregorian autocracy frightened many of us even more than the notion of a MAGA takeover!

Zed's survival was entirely due to Leo's genius. Much to Gregory's annoyance, Leo evolved an alternative defensive strategy which required a depth of understanding far beyond Gregory's abilities. But Zed would allow no new initiative without the approval of his trusted Head of Security, Krebs. Gregory pestered Krebs to block any suggestions from Leo. "We don't even know if he is Leo or Leonie. And he comes from MAGA land. How can we trust him?" But Krebs watched the video of our being entertained by the Planet of the Apes remake and Leo's subsequent eviction from the land of his birth. If anything, Krebs was more suspicious of Gregory than Leo. So, he allowed Leo to speak directly with the President.

Leo explained to Zed that there would be no defence dome as this would almost certainly be penetrated.

Instead, Leo could protect the President if he were allowed to take blood samples from Zed. From these he would construct an entirely fake molecular image of the President. Zed's own image projection would be obscured leaving the fake image open to attack. Sure enough, the MAGA attack saw swarms of merones destroy the fake. MAGA observers knew that the attack had been successful yet, the next day, Zed was more alive than ever.

It was a week after this brilliant coup that I met Leo. He was dressed as Leonie and was dancing in the Dionysus gay club. Zed's pathological hatred of homosexuality did not extend to closing the club where he knew his saviour would hang out for relaxation. On the contrary, there were several poorly disguised, heavily armed guards surrounding the building in case anyone tried to take down Zed's star scientist. Even Krebs himself could be seen surveying the dancers from a vantage point. Perhaps he would have liked to join the dance?

Of course, Leo did not think of himself as a scientist. Like Xavier, he regarded the intramolecular realm within which he worked and roamed as the visible location of the archetypal structures that underpinned what we perceived as "reality". Others in the club declared themselves convinced by voodoo and other animalist beliefs. But Leo, like his father, refused to follow this well-trodden path. He (or she) talked to me at the bar in the club about how these archetypal structures pervade our dreams as well as what we believe to be the 'real world'. "I loved my father and his delving into the substructure of life opened the way for us to understand the Universe in which we live and die," he said to me. "But you know that those who took his words literally concerning water, wood and the crucifixion are as foolhardy as those who believe in the literal translation of the many holy texts that we are taught. Do you know that the fundamentalists who support the mad MAGA honestly believe that he will live for eternity provided they can erase all water and wood from the intramolecular universe within which they dream. They have gone about destroying all trace of water and wood so that his projected image cannot be crucified!"

"So, what will happen to him?" I asked.

"You will see his fate in a collective dream in the coming month. I am sure." And, with that, Leonie skipped away and started dancing with a graceful man who had, no doubt, been thoroughly checked over by Krebs.

The International Celebration of Xavier's Life and Work was due to take place in Oslo. Brilliant scientists and metaphysicians attended, and Leo was a star speaker. Zed allowed him to go provided he was accompanied by a small army of guards with an array of weaponry usually only on display for the autocrats themselves. Leo left strict instructions with Krebs that no one should be allowed access to Zed without the protective screen that could only be operated from within the President's own private study. Michael Mayer (or MM as he was known) had been one of Xavier's star pupils: but in Oslo he presented a MAGA-based theory that Leo described as absurd. "You fail to grasp Xavier's insight that the crucifixion is primary and that it will find any way by which to become manifest. By deleting water and tree, you simply invite alternative manifestations."

One of MM's fundamentalist followers objected to Leo. "You are just a pawn in Zed's game. You should not be here. You will say anything to deny the possibility that we can achieve eternal life for MAGA. He will not be crucified because we will prevent that fate within the confines of the molecular universe within which we are now the masters."

"That idiot doesn't even understand how immersion into the crucifixion archetype guarantees some form of existence beyond an individual's physical death," Leo commented to his guards who had no idea what Leo was talking about.

Gregory's coordinated assault upon the MAGA presidency was timed to coincide with MM's absence in

Oslo. The launch of thousands of merones within the vicinity of the victim were countered by MM's impressive ion dome defence. Over ninety five percent of the merones were destroyed: but the five percent that evaded the ions were more than enough to kill the man. The world's press and social media largely presented this assassination as the response to the attempt upon Zed that had been totally countered by Leo's defence. And, just as Leo predicted, many of the MAGA followers reported a collective dream in which they saw their hero strung up roughly within a latticework of metal scaffold bars – with no wood nor water anywhere to be seen.

Leo's return from Oslo was marred by a crude attempt on his life. The aircraft in which he was travelling was forced to make an emergency landing when a sabotage explosive failed to ignite. Krebs met Leo the moment he arrived home with news that there had been another attempt upon Zed.

"We don't know how the attacker evaded your defensive device. How is it possible?"

Leo surveyed the data sets and pointed to a telltale eruption of figures whose presence was unexpected. "That is an entry into Zed's private molecular space. Whoever made that entry must have planted the disruptor which could kill our leader."

Gregory told Krebs that he suspected Leo. But Krebs

knew that Leo had already saved Zed's life once before and, anyway, the attack was carried out when Leo was in Oslo. Zed, feeling very ill, and Krebs, looking very harassed, met with Leo to ask how to identify the intruder.

"That's very simple," Leo asserted. "Present that plume of data that accompanied the intruder upon entry into the identification funnel. It's the same one you use for identifying anyone requesting entry into the palace. You will obtain a clear image of their face and a readout of their DNA. I will bet my last paycheck that it will be the same person who ordered the bomb to be planted in my aircraft coming home."

When Krebs shared the readout with Zed, the president was incandescent with rage. "I knew that Gregory was ambitious: but to want to murder his own flesh and blood!"

--

The next morning the Dionysus was buzzing. Rumours surged and receded; no one really knew what was happening. It was thought that Gregory had fled the capital and was hiding out in one of the ecclesiastical palaces, protected by his close ally, Archbishop Nicholas.

When Leonie arrived, she caused a stir. Dressed in an

immaculate silk dress and sporting a voluptuous, blond wig, she came and sat down near our little band of image recognition technicians and scientists. Krebs himself could be seen directing his men to create a protective ring around our table. The archbishop had issued a notice strongly implying that Leo was somehow behind the attempt upon Zed and that the case against Gregory was a foul MAGA slander. Krebs regarded this as a desperate act to save Gregory. After all, as the assault was taking place, thousands of delegates and a massive posse of his own guards were watching Leo perform in Oslo.

"You are looking very beautiful today," I commented to Leonie. She smiled at me, her fellow fugitive from MAGA after the fury created by the Planet of the Apes remake. "Come and dance with me," she said.

Dozens of couples were on the dance floor: but they made way for us. I whispered in her ear: "how did you do it?"

She began pirouetting and suddenly stopping with a jerk to point at the floor behind me. Then she repeated the manoeuvre but pointed at the floor behind her. I was unsure of what she was trying to say. But after a couple of twists, I realised she was pointing at our shadows.

"Shadow!" I said under my breath.

She nodded and called out a word that sounded like

"young" but then I understood she was trying to make me focus upon the word "shadow" within the conceptions laid out by "Jung". She laughed when she saw that I understood but gave no further clues in case others twigged what she was telling me. A few minutes later, she made a dramatic exit, plunging through the back door supported by a small troupe of dancers who had accompanied her throughout the performance.

There was a sudden stir as an announcer entered the club. Normally, governmental announcers only made pronouncements online or via tv and radio. But this one walked to the stage and silence fell across the room.

"A few minutes ago, despite all that our best physicians could do, our beloved leader, President Zed, passed away. No stone will be left unturned to discover how he was killed, and the perpetrator will not escape justice. As a sign of respect, this club and the others that opened this morning will be closed until further notice."

As we filed out, I could see Krebs talking to the announcer. He was agitated and gesticulating wildly. I hoped that an unstable Krebs did not spell danger to Leo or any of us whom he might suspect of treachery. Innocence, as we had seen, was no protection against a furious but perplexed security chief. But the truth was that Krebs regarded Leo as the one true, loyal guardian of his leader because of his initial action in diverting the

MAGA merone attack. Krebs hated the pontificating archbishop and the fact that Nicholas was shielding the strongest suspect in Zed's death had him pressing the announcer to declare Gregory as the most wanted man on the run.

In the event, Krebs never got his hands on Gregory. Thinking he was safe within the confines of the great cathedral was a sad error of judgement. Known as the driver of the merone attack that had killed the MAGA leader, a revenge assault was made against him by the Michael Mayerson team. He died holding his head and falling back onto the altar, a "sacrificial lamb" according to the archbishop, keen to retain some religious significance to the man's death. But this untimely demise left Krebs with many unanswered questions.

The spectacular dance that Leonie had used to cover what she hoped was a secret message did not fool Krebs. Although he could not understand what was being said, he knew that there had been a message and was determined to discover what it was and what it meant. To mislead an intelligent analyst like Krebs, it was always best to keep as near the truth as possible. I realised that the reference to the Jung archetype, shadow, would have been worked out even before questioning, I hoped I was prepared for the interview carried out by Krebs himself.

"What was Leo telling you in the club?"

"This was Leo's alter ego, Leonie, so she likes working in riddles and artistic poses. But I think I worked out what she was saying on behalf of Leo."

"Well, tell me what she said."

I took a deep breath and paused. I hoped that this would convince Krebs that I was coming clean about the entire message. I asked for a drink of water and Krebs shouted to one of the guards to bring in a carafe. Once I had taken a sip, I went on with my tale.

"Leonie wanted me to understand the word 'shadow' in a very specific context. She knew that in my face recognition work I would have had to study all the various theories about underlying structures that usually determine exactly what it is we see. So, she shouted a word that, at first, I thought was 'young'. But that didn't make sense. We know exactly how old Zed and all our leading players are. But then I wondered whether the word she was trying to articulate was 'Jung'. Are you following what I'm saying?"

Krebs nodded and I knew that I had told him nothing he had not already worked out for himself.

"In Jungian theory, shadow has a very specific meaning. It is an archetype. But its significance alters between people. Shadow for me is not shadow for you. So, what was shadow for Zed? That was the question whose answer would tell us everything that Leo knew."

I paused again because I wanted to gauge how much

of this Krebs had already surmised. It seemed to me this was as far as he had reached and that my honesty so far should put me in good stead when it came to my interpretation.

"Go on. Don't stop there!" Krebs was becoming excited. This was a good sign.

"My understanding of shadow – and you can check this out with any of our psychologist specialists – is that it is a bit like the contents of Pandora's tin or box. All the fears and troubles that you have are contained therein and it remains as a constant thorn in the mind, pricking away with nowhere else to go. It is an archetype, so it cannot go away. It is a permanent feature of each of our universes. So, what was in Zed's shadow. What was the fear that would never leave him? Whatever it was points to where the attack originated. I think I know what Leo saw as Zed's shadow."

"You can prove this?" Krebs interjected.

I shook my head. "There can be no proof now because even a deep trance analysis of Zed's fears undertaken whilst he was under hypnosis is no longer available to us. But I think that Leo saw Zed's deepest shadow as betrayal."

Krebs and I sat in silence whilst he digested this interpretation. He was thinking about Zed as his boss, as his friend, as the nation's disputed leader and of those who might represent a challenge. Eventually, he nodded.

"I have no idea why Leo has to put on all this make up and female attire. Couldn't he just have told us what you have just told me?"

I shrugged my shoulders. "I'm not a performance artist. I'm just an analyst so I don't really understand how his temperament works. But he is the creative. He is the only one to have evolved an effective defence against merones. He saved Zed against the MAGA threat but could not be here defending Zed against someone so close to him whilst speaking to the rest of the world in Oslo. I know Gregory and the archbishop were accusing Leo of this crime, but I do not believe a word they say.

Krebs nodded. "No. Nor do I. You can go now. Thank you for telling me all you know. Do you think I could discover more from interviewing Leo himself?"

"I'm sure you will try but my only fear is that he will transform into Leonie and annoy you for appearing to be evasive. But you know that, at heart, he is on our side and may have more insight into what our enemies are planning than any of us by dreaming and imagining scenarios that we cannot grasp yet."

--

Krebs was woken up the next morning by a shout from Leo. He had had the cheek and initiative to visit Krebs at his home before the investigator called him in.

"What do you want?" Krebs was slightly annoyed, but Leo had him on the back foot.

"We need to establish a video link to Michael Mayerson urgently. We can bring this war to a successful conclusion: but only if I can speak directly to Mayerson. I know him well. He will be at a loss what to do next, but I am already a step or two ahead of him."

Krebs was about to object, but Leo walked away quickly and shouted: "I'll call you later as I need to prepare now."

That afternoon saw Leo with a very small group of us sitting in a study awaiting the video feed to go live. When it buzzed into life, we could see Mayerson in a huge operations room surrounded by dozens of technicians, security guards, software specialists (some of whom I knew) and psych experts brought in to advise on how to deal with Leo. Leo sat with just a couple of face recognition people, an interpreter (if needed) and Krebs. He assured us that he could deal with "poor Michael".

Leo had warned Krebs that Mayerson's team would attempt to convince Krebs that Leo was the criminal who had killed his leader. "He will first try to sow division amongst his enemies. You need to pretend to be listening and, eventually, it will be my turn to speak. That is when the meeting proper will begin and we shall see how they react. I suspect that they will be shocked and may even disbelieve what I can do as they have no idea how to manipulate deep molecular structures. But they will have to learn." Krebs nodded and Leo asked me and the other face recognition specialists to watch Mayerson for telltale facial expressions that would guide us in deciding how to deal with him.

The meeting began exactly as Leo had predicted. Mayerson asked Leo how he had managed to murder Zed. "Congratulations, Leo, in pretending to save him one day just so that you would have the opportunity to kill him and Gregory a few days later."

Leo smiled and said he appreciated Michael's professional praise for his achievements but that was not the main reason why we were having the meeting.

"You see, Michael, the question is not how to murder people with merones. What you and I need to agree is how to prevent people from being murdered. Otherwise, this tit for tat war could go one forever. I am sure you agree."

Leo looked to us for an assessment as to how Mayerson was reacting. "I think he is unsure. He doesn't know where you are going in this," I whispered in his ear. Leo nodded.

"Now I know that whatever verbal or written assurance I give you, or you give me, will be regarded with scepticism. So, without consulting you or other security focused personnel, I decided to act on my own and believe I may have resolved the problem finally.”

“How could you have done that?” a disbelieving security guard sitting beside Mayerson interjected.

“I’m sorry,” Leo said, “I don’t think I know you. Are you a specialist in molecular deep structures? If not, perhaps you will allow me to talk with Michael Mayerson who is one of the world’s experts.”

Mayerson pushed the man aside. “What have you done Leo?” he asked.

“It is all a question of which is the appropriate deep structure to engage when an attack is about to take place.”

“What do you mean?”

“Well, Michael, I have rearranged the substructure.”

“What! How have you done that?”

“An explanation of how my practice has developed so much further will have to wait until later. Meanwhile, let me explain what will happen if anyone attempts any form of merone attack, anywhere in the world against anyone – and that includes people who live here in our country. I have organised the substructure to engage one and only one archetype. You will recognise it as the ouroboros, the snake biting its tail.”

Mayerson spun round and started talking with his psych experts. He was clearly unclear as to what Leo’s actions would mean. Eventually, he turned back and said: “My team believe that what you have done is to set up a structured guarantee that anyone launching an attack would be attacking themselves. Is that correct?"

"Your experts are to be congratulated. That is precisely what would happen."

"So, if we launch an assault on you and you take no defensive manoeuvre, the attacker will be committing suicide."

"Exactly."

"Do you want us to attempt to kill you?"

"Of course not. I am simply saying that if any loyal soldier from your impressive armed forces were to try to kill me with merones, he would die the moment he launched the attack, and I would remain unscathed."

A huge bull of a man in battledress pressed forward, pushing Mayerson aside. He was shouting but until he reached Mayerson's microphone, we could not make out his words. Finally, we heard him scream: "you cannot take this girlie seriously. He dresses in a frock and thinks he can outbluff a soldier. This joker knows damn well that I have an advanced merone contingent surrounding his venue. Now he believes that he can scare us into downing our weapon. But my men on the ground need do nothing as I can launch the fastest merone ever constructed straight at the back of his head, right now."

The tiny, handheld control was slammed onto the table, as if the man believed he had won a high money round of poker. The launch button was banged down and a zip sound screeched through the room.

The era of the Autocrats ended with General Trumpington Water's decapitation.

HOPE

It is September when insects become drowsy. My son, George, was poking around a wasp nest and would not stop until I told him this story.

"Listen as I tell you how Zeus punished mankind after the Titan Prometheus stole the secret of fire from the gods. In retribution he created Pandora to become the wife of Prometheus's brother, Epimetheus. Ignoring Prometheus's warnings, Epimetheus brought Pandora home together with the wedding gift provided by Zeus. The gift was a storage jar containing all the evils of this world which escaped when Pandora innocently opened it.

The jar was much later renamed a 'box' by Erasmus – presumably because it was easier to imagine the lid of a box being opened then shut quickly which would have permitted just one grace, hope, to remain. Perhaps, since the acquisition of 'sfika' (Σφήκα translated as 'wasp' from the Greek), all we have left in this world is hope.

Now, my son, the knowledge that we have of killing fellow human beings has reached extraordinary depths during modern warfare. But it was not until the creation of a sfika that a terrifying glimpse of the future was revealed – if only we had not ignored the warnings. The first sfika was created in Greece using a 3-d printer.

Powered by a miniscule and dirt cheap 'motor', it flew with tiny 'wings' that made it look just like a wasp. The first developers saw it as a possible observation vehicle – like a very small drone. But just as drones became used as weapons, the sfika began its inevitable ascent (or descent) into becoming the ultimate instrument of war.

It may have looked like a wasp, but the sfika had the capacity to carry very basic artificial intelligence capacity in its observation eye. The first use in a battle was almost useless. It flew towards enemy lines carrying a small explosive charge, eyeing its target remorselessly. But as it moved quite slowly, a soldier could bat it away as if playing baseball. The sfika would explode harmlessly nowhere near its target. If only we had given up on its development at that stage, we would not be where we are now.

The next two developments catapulted the sfika into becoming what we now recognise as the ultimate killing machine. Artificial intelligence capacity combined with access to 3-d printing gave strategists the idea that the sfika could reproduce itself. By producing hundreds, or thousands, of these 'wasps', it became almost impossible for soldiers to destroy them all before detonation. And so, their use on the frontline became normal. Again, if only we had stopped there, we may have been satisfied with our innovative skills. But the second development utilised the sfika 'brain' by programming the picture and profile of the individual commander of opposing troops. The sfika horde set out with just one target. When he was spotted, they swarmed over him, killing him with the combination of tiny explosives.

We are uncertain which nation decided to use the easily produced sfikas for assassination. Instead of explosives, a tiny 'wasp sting' of cyanide was carried and soon, the deaths of leading politicians, controversial celebrities (and even random individuals killed through sfika flight failures) made sfika production illegal in most countries. That made almost no difference as every country decided to maintain sfika capacity as a deterrent threat to the leader of any country intending to attack them.

It has been some years now since any nation has gone to war with another. Land disputes cannot be settled by military means without the almost inevitable death of the leaders of both nations. The acquisition of sfikas by organised crime syndicates was a major concern until opposition syndicates (as well as 'unofficial' police units) started using them. Some say we are now in the "happy" position of mutual deterrence ensuring peaceful coexistence. Others regard our existence as precarious and, like Epimetheus, find that there is just one thing remaining in the jar – and that is hope.

So, George, as you were poking that wasp's nest in our garden this morning, my one hope was that you'd not disturbed and been stung by a random roaming sfika.

MY FRIENDS

I have lived a long time. Many of my friends, older than
me, have died. None were more gracious than Wesley
and Ahmed.

They were like rarely parted brothers. Wesley was a
deeply religious Quaker, the most conscientious, gentle,
pacifist I have ever known. His devoted wife, Penelope,
had given him a son, Otto, who did not share his
father's beliefs. Even before the event for which the
family became known, Penelope was torn between her
son and husband in matters of religion and politics.

Otto was a moody child. Wesley tried to engage him
in sports, in travel, in anything that might persuade him
to stop playing computer games or reading internet
rubbish on his phone. But nothing seemed to interest
him. At school he was poor academically but liked
contact sports – he was a half decent footballer whose
one failing was a tendency to blame his mistakes on
other team members.

Ahmed was a soldier. Somehow, he balanced his
Taoist upbringing against his duties as a trained
marksman. I was fascinated when listening to him
debating with Wesley about how to respond to the
threats to our liberal, democratic civilisation from what
they described as far-right thugs, billionaire financiers
of far-right thugs, and self-righteous politicians

supported by oligarchs, far-right right thugs and their easily duped neighbours.

Ahmed admitted that his pacifist upbringing made his first response to those espousing far-right, fascist opinions was to engage them in debate to try to alter their views with facts and reason. But, as he put it, if push came to shove, he knew that if it came to a fight, he would never hesitate to use his skills as a soldier. Wesley, on the other hand, argued that violence of any sort could only result in more violence. He would cite Gandhi and Martin Luther King as his models. "Non-violent resistance is the only long-term resolution to any armed conflict".

I can still hear him saying those words. Yet when his son came marching into the house in full neo-Nazi uniform, shouting slogans learnt from social media influencers and physically confronting his father, Wesley (according to Penelope) resisted by pushing him away. Otto fell back and sustained a severe head wound from which he never recovered.

It was not the severity of his son's injury that broke Wesley. It was not even the subsequent breakup of his marriage to Penelope who spent the rest of her life tending to her son. It was his failure as a pacifist that only Ahmed appreciated. Otto's supporters were a ragtag bunch of rough boys ruled by a middle-aged man who would hold forth espousing conspiracy theories and a variety of racist, homophobic and xenophobic views. He was regarded as their leader because he was a practicing lawyer. It was he who persuaded Otto to sue his father for assault and attempted murder. The case attracted media attention, little interest from the judge who dismissed the case within days but acted as a key pressure pushing Penelope and Wesley further apart.

And now, over a decade after both my friends and Penelope have died, Otto's much-detested State is his sole guardian, paying for the daily assistance he requires just to stay alive. Yet the forces that drove him to confront his dad are still very active and show little sign of retreat. And my friends have left us with the same dilemma: if it is not in the selfish self-interests of powerful, wealthy men to respond to appeals of reason and kindness, are we only left with Wesley's reflexive push with all its tragic consequences?